For everyone who has
felt fairy magic

Special thanks to
Sue Bentley

No part of this publication may be reproduced
in whole or in part, or stored in a retrieval
system, or transmitted in any form or by any
means, electronic, mechanical, photocopying,
recording, or otherwise, without written permission
of the publisher. For information regarding
permission, write to Working Partners Limited,
1 Albion Place, London W6 OQT, United Kingdom.

ISBN 0-439-69192-3

12   14 15 16/0

Printed in the U.S.A.

First printing, March 2005

Heather the Violet Fairy

by Daisy Meadows
illustrated by Georgie Ripper

SCHOLASTIC INC.

New York Toronto London Auckland Sydney
Mexico City New Delhi Hong Kong Buenos Aires

The Fairyland Palace

Maze

Forest

Orchard

Black Pot

Meadow

Tower

Beach

Rock pools

Rainspell Island

Shells

Cold winds blow and thick ice forms,
I conjure up this fairy storm.
To seven corners of the mortal world
the Rainbow Fairies will be hurled!

I curse every part of Fairyland,
with a frosty wave of my icy hand.
For now and always, from this fateful day,
Fairyland will be cold and gray!

All the Rainbow Fairies are together
except one! The fairies will never get
their Rainbow Magic back without
Heather the **Violet Fairy**

Contents

Message on a Kite

"I can't believe this is the last day of our vacation!" said Rachel Walker. She gazed up at her kite as it rose in the clear blue sky.

Kirsty Tate watched the purple kite soar above the field beside Mermaid Cottage. "But we still have to find Heather!" she reminded Rachel.

Jack Frost's wicked spell had banished the seven Rainbow Fairies to Rainspell Island. And without the Rainbow Fairies, Fairyland had no color! Kirsty and Rachel had already found Ruby, Amber, Sunny, Fern, Sky, and Inky. Now there was just Heather the Violet Fairy left to find.

Rachel felt the kite tug on its string. She looked up. Something violet and silver flashed at the end of the kite's long tail. "Look up there!" she shouted.

Kirsty shaded her eyes with her hand. "What is it? Do you think it's a fairy?" she asked.

"I'm not sure," Rachel said, winding in the string.

As the kite came bobbing toward them, Kirsty saw that a long piece of violet-colored ribbon was tied to its tail. She helped Rachel untie the ribbon and smooth it out.

"It has tiny silver writing on it," Rachel said.

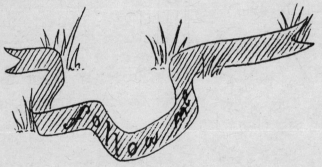

Kirsty crouched down to have a closer look. "It says, *Follow me*."

Suddenly, the ribbon was lifted up by the breeze. It fluttered across the field.

"It must be leading us to Heather!" Kirsty said, jumping up.

Rachel rolled up her kite. "Mom, is it OK if we go exploring one last time?" she called.

Mrs. Walker was talking to Kirsty's mom in the yard outside Mermaid Cottage. Kirsty's family was staying in Dolphin Cottage, next door. "Of course, as long as Kirsty's mom agrees," Mrs. Walker replied.

"It's fine by me," said Mrs. Tate. "But don't go far. The ferry leaves at four o'clock."

"We'll have to hurry!" Rachel whispered to Kirsty.

They ran through the soft, green grass,
following the ribbon, which bobbed and
drifted on the breeze.

Suddenly, the ribbon whisked out of
sight behind a thick hedge.

"Where's it gone?" Kirsty wondered.

"Through here!" Rachel said, pulling
aside one of the branches.

Kirsty followed her friend as she
squeezed through the hedge. Luckily, the
leaves weren't too prickly. On the other
side they found a path, and a gate. There
was a sign on the gate, in purple paint,
saying: SUMMER FAIR TODAY!

Kirsty and Rachel went through the gate and into a pretty garden. Stalls were selling cotton candy and ice cream at the edge of a smooth, green lawn. There were people everywhere, chatting and laughing.

"Isn't this great?" Rachel said, looking around in surprise. A woman with a little girl holding a bunch of balloons smiled at her.

Suddenly, Kirsty spotted the ribbon fluttering toward a merry-go-round at the far end of the lawn. It wrapped itself around the golden flagpole and danced in the breeze like a tiny flag. "It must be leading us to the merry-go-round!" Kirsty said. She grabbed her friend's hand and they ran across the grass. The merry-go-round was as pretty as a fairy castle. Rachel stared with delight at the circle of wooden horses on their shiny golden poles.

"Hello there!" called a friendly voice behind them. "I'm Tom Goodfellow. Do you like my merry-go-round?"

Rachel and Kirsty turned to see an old man with white hair and a kind smile. "Yes, it's lovely," Rachel said.

Kirsty watched the wooden horses rising and falling in time to the cheerful music. "Look, Rachel." She gasped. "The horses are all rainbow colors! Red, orange, yellow, green, blue, indigo, and violet."

Rachel looked closer. Through the
whirling horses, she could see that the
pillar in the center of the merry-go-round
was decorated with a picture of rainbow-
colored horses galloping along a beach.

The merry-go-round slowed down and the music stopped. Mr. Goodfellow climbed up to help the riders dismount. "All aboard for the next ride!" he called. Lots more excited children began to climb up onto the horses.

Mr. Goodfellow smiled down at Rachel and Kirsty. "How about you two?" he asked, his blue eyes twinkling.

A Magical Ride

"We'd love to have a ride on your merry-go-round!" said Kirsty. "Quick, Rachel, there are two horses left!" She scrambled up onto one of them. A name was painted, in gold, on the saddle. "My horse is called Indigo Princess," Kirsty said, stroking the horse's shiny coat.

Rachel climbed onto a pretty
horse next to Kirsty's. It had
a lilac-colored coat and
a silver mane. "Mine
is called Prancing
Violet."

"Hold tight,
everyone!" Mr.
Goodfellow
called out.

The music
started up and
the merry-go-
round began to
turn. Prancing Violet
and Indigo Princess
swooped up and down
on their painted poles.

Rachel laughed out loud as the ride

spun faster and faster. The garden flashed by, and the flowers and paths disappeared in a blur. The sounds of music and laughter faded away. Rachel's heart skipped a beat. Now, the only horse she could see was Kirsty's horse, Indigo Princess. And she could feel Prancing Violet's hooves thudding on the ground beneath her. Kirsty felt a sea breeze tugging at her hair. Indigo Princess seemed to toss her head and kick up sand as she galloped along.

"Oh!" Kirsty exclaimed, tasting salt spray on her lips. "This is like riding a real horse!"

"It's awesome!" Rachel agreed. She felt as if they were racing along a beach, just like the horses she'd seen on the pillar in the middle of the merry-go-round.

But before Rachel could say anything else, the horses began to slow down. The sandy beach faded away, and the sound of music returned. The merry-go-round came to a smooth halt.

Kirsty patted Indigo Princess's neck as she dismounted. "Thanks for the special ride!" she whispered. Then she turned to Rachel. "This merry-go-round is definitely magical, but where is Heather the Violet Fairy?"

Rachel slipped out of Prancing Violet's saddle and frowned. "I don't know," she said. Then she heard the tiniest tinkling laugh. It was coming from behind her. Rachel turned around. There was nobody there, just the picture on the pillar in the middle of the merry-go-round.

Rachel blinked. There was a fairy riding the violet-colored horse! She wore a short, floaty, purple dress, long purple stockings, and ballet slippers. A few purple flowers were tucked behind one of her ears.

"Kirsty!" Rachel whispered, pointing. "I think I've just found Heather the Violet Fairy!"

The Seventh Fairy

Mr. Goodfellow was helping the other riders off the horses. Quickly, Rachel and Kirsty squeezed past the other horses to look more closely at the pillar.

"Heather must be trapped in the painting!" Rachel said.

"We've got to get her out!" Kirsty said.

"Yes," Rachel agreed. "But how, and what can we do with all these people here?"

Just then, almost as if he had heard them, Mr. Goodfellow clapped his hands. "Follow me, everyone. The clowns are here!"

A cheer went up as everyone scrambled off the merry-go-round. All the other children ran across the lawn toward the clowns, so Rachel and Kirsty were left alone.

"Now's our chance!" Kirsty said.

Rachel had an idea. "I know! Let's use our magic bags," she said. Titania, the Fairy Queen, had given Kirsty and Rachel bags of special gifts to help them rescue the Rainbow Fairies.

"Of course! I've got mine here." Kirsty put her hand in her pocket and took out her magic bag. It was glowing with a soft, golden light. When she opened it, a cloud of glitter fizzed up into the air.

Kirsty slipped her hand into the bag. There was something there, long and slim like a pencil. It was a tiny golden paintbrush.

Kirsty felt puzzled. "What help is that? We don't want to paint any *more* pictures."

"Maybe Heather knows what we can use it for," Rachel suggested. "Amber told us how to help her when she was trapped in the shell."

"Good idea," Kirsty said. As she bent closer to the pillar, the tip of the brush touched the painted fairy's hand.

Suddenly, the whole picture glowed, and the fairy's tiny fingers moved! A single violet-scented petal floated down from the picture. "Look!" Rachel gasped. "The brush is working some magic on the painting!" Kirsty whispered.

She began to stroke the brush all
around the outline of the fairy.

At first, nothing seemed to happen.
Then, the picture glowed
even brighter. The fairy
shivered. "That tickles!"
she said with a silvery
laugh.

The magic brush
had painted Heather
back to life!

Rachel checked to see
that no one was watching
them. Then, with Kirsty's
last stroke, the fairy sprang
out of the painting, her wings
flashing like jewels. Purple fairy dust shot
everywhere, turning into violet-scented
blossoms that floated around her.

"Thank you so much for rescuing me!"
said Heather, hovering in front of them.
She held a purple wand, tipped with
silver. "I'm Heather the Violet Fairy! Who
are you? Do you know where my
Rainbow sisters are?"

"I'm Rachel, and this is Kirsty," said
Rachel. "Your sisters are all safe in the
pot-at-the-end-of-the-rainbow."

"Hooray!" Heather
did a twirl
of delight,
scattering
violet sparks
around them.
"I can't wait to
see them again."
Kirsty held out her
hand and Heather

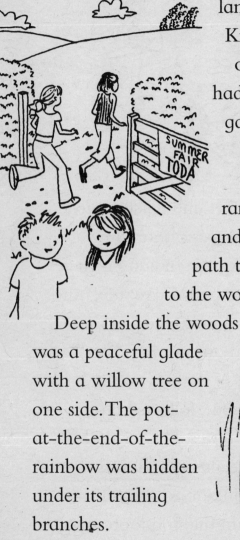

landed gently on it. Kirsty held her out of view until they had run through the garden, past all the people watching the clowns. They ran out of the gate, and down the path that led to the woods.

Deep inside the woods was a peaceful glade with a willow tree on one side. The pot-at-the-end-of-the-rainbow was hidden under its trailing branches.

As soon as Rachel and Kirsty reached the clearing, there was a shout from inside the pot. Inky the Indigo Fairy zoomed out. "Heather! You're safe!" she cried. "Look, everybody! Rachel and Kirsty have found our missing sister!"

Sunny flew out of the pot on the back of a huge bumblebee, followed by the other Rainbow Fairies. The air flashed and fizzed with scented bubbles, flowers and leaves, stars, inkdrops, and tiny butterflies. Bertram the frog footman

hopped out from behind the pot, a smile
from ear to ear on his broad, green face.

As the fairies flew up to hug and kiss
Heather, her blossom-filled fairy dust
mingled with theirs, and the scent of
violets filled the clearing.

"We *knew* you were coming,"
said Amber the Orange
Fairy, doing a cartwheel.
"I've been tingly with
magic all morning!"

Rachel and Kirsty held hands and danced in a circle. They'd done it! They had found all seven Rainbow Fairies!

"And who is this?" Heather asked Sunny the Yellow Fairy, reaching out to tickle the queen bee under her chin.

"This is Queenie," said Sunny, kissing the bee's furry head. "She rescued my wand after the goblins stole it."

Ruby the Red Fairy's
wings sparkled as she
fluttered down to
land on Rachel's
shoulder. "Thank
you, Rachel and
Kirsty," she said.

"You are true
fairy friends,"
agreed Fern the Green
Fairy, drifting onto Kirsty's hand. "And
now that we're all
together again,
we must use
magic to make
a rainbow to
take us back
to Fairyland."

Suddenly, Rachel heard a strange crackling sound. She spun around. The pond at the edge of the glade wasn't blue anymore. It was white and cloudy with ice! Rachel and Kirsty and the fairies stared at one another in alarm.

"Goblins!" they cried. Sky the Blue Fairy shivered with fright and fluttered closer to Sunny and Queenie.

Inky's tiny teeth chattered. "B-b-but it can't be. The Sugarplum Fairy kept them in the Land of Sweets, harvesting jelly beans!"

Just then, a harsh, cackling laugh rang out. The bushes parted, and a tall, bony fairy walked into the glade. Icicles hung from his clothes and there was frost on his white hair and eyebrows.

It was Jack Frost!

Fairy Spells

"So, you are all together again!" Jack Frost's angry voice sounded like icicles snapping.

"Yes, thanks to Rachel and Kirsty," Ruby declared bravely. "And now we want to go home to Fairyland!"

Jack Frost gave a laugh like hailstones spattering against a windowpane. "I will

never allow that!" he told them. But before
Jack Frost could point his evil finger,

Ruby the Red Fairy flew high
into the air. "Come on,
Rainbow Fairies! Now
that we're together
again, all our Rainbow
Magic powers have
come back. This time,
we must try to stop
him with a spell.
Follow me!" she called.

Immediately, Inky shot to her sister's
side, and turned to face Jack Frost with
her hands on her hips and a determined
look on her face. The other fairy sisters
flew to join them, and they all lifted their
wands, chanting together:

*"To protect the Rainbow Fairies all,
Make a magic raindrop wall!"*

Kirsty held Rachel's hand, feeling very
scared. Would the spell work?

A rainbow-colored spray shot out of
each wand and a shining wall of raindrops
appeared. It hung like a waterfall
between the fairies and Jack Frost.

Rachel and Kirsty held their breath.

"It will take more than a few raindrops to stop me!" Jack Frost hissed. He pointed one bony finger at the shimmering wall.

At once, the raindrops turned to ice. They dropped onto the frosty grass like tiny glass beads and shattered.

All the fairies looked horrified. Sunny
and Sky gave sobs of dismay and Inky
clenched her fists. Fern, Amber, and Ruby
hugged one another tightly. Heather
hovered at one side, looking as if she was
thinking hard.

Rachel and Kirsty stared in alarm as Jack Frost lifted his hand again.

Then Heather flew forward, waved her wand, and cried:

"To stop Jack Frost
from causing trouble,
Catch him in a magic bubble!"

A gleaming bubble popped out of the end of Heather's wand. It grew bigger and bigger. It looked as if it was made of pale lilac glass. Jack Frost started to laugh, and stretched out his icy fingers. But before he could do anything, there was a loud fizzing sound. Jack Frost vanished.

Rachel blinked.

Heather's spell had trapped Jack Frost *inside* the bubble! It bobbed gently down onto the grass. The wicked fairy pressed his hands against the shiny wall and looked furious.

"Oh, great job, Heather!" Fern exclaimed.

"Quick, everyone. We must get into the pot-at-the-end-of-the-rainbow and make a rainbow to take us back to Fairyland!" Heather urged. "Jack Frost still might escape!"

Rachel and Kirsty held the branches of the willow tree out of the way so that the fairies could fly through.

Heather's tiny eyebrows shot
up as a squirrel skittered
down the willow tree's
trunk, toward the pot.
"Who are you?" she
asked.

"This is Fluffy," said
Fern, stroking the squirrel.
"He helped me escape from the
goblins."

"Fluffy and Queenie will have to go
back to their homes now," said Sky sadly.

"Can't they live with you in
Fairyland?" Rachel asked.

"No, they have their own homes to go
back to," Fern explained. "But we'll
come and visit them, won't we?" All the
fairies nodded and Sunny wiped away
a tiny tear.

Fern reached up to give Fluffy one last hug. Her sisters fluttered around, giving Queenie and Fluffy little kisses and hugs.

"Thank you again for all your help," said Ruby.

Queenie buzzed good-bye as she flew away. Fluffy gave a farewell flick of his tail, then scampered off.

Heather fluttered in front of Rachel and Kirsty. "Would you like to come to Fairyland with us? I'm sure Queen Titania and King Oberon will want to thank you."

Rachel and Kirsty nodded eagerly. Heather smiled and waved her wand, sprinkling the girls with purple fairy dust.

Kirsty felt herself shrinking. The grass seemed to rush toward her. "Hooray! I'm a fairy again!" she cried.

Rachel laughed in delight as wings sprang from her shoulders.

Just then, there was a yell from the giant bubble.

Rachel and Kirsty looked around.

Jack Frost was looking very scared. His face was bright red and drops of water ran down his cheeks. He was *melting*!

"Well, he can't stop you from getting to Fairyland now," said Kirsty. But Sky's wings drooped. She hovered in the air, looking sad. "Without Jack Frost, there will be no seasons. We need his cold and ice to make winter," she pointed out.

"No winter?" Inky said, looking shocked. "But I love sledding in the snow and skating on the frozen river."

"Without winter, how can spring follow?" Amber said in a small voice. "What will happen to all the lovely spring flowers?"

"And the bees need the flowers to make honey in summer," Sunny said sadly.

"After summer, autumn comes. The squirrels find nuts to store for hibernation then," said Fern.

"We have to have all the seasons, you see. If we leave Jack Frost in that bubble . . ."

The fairies looked upset. Then, Heather spoke up. "This is all true. But most importantly, I feel sorry for Jack Frost. He looks very frightened."

"Heather's right. We have to do something," said Ruby.

"But he might cast another spell!" Kirsty said.

"Even so, we have to help him, don't we?" Amber said firmly. And all the other Rainbow Fairies agreed.

Kirsty felt so proud of them. The kind fairies were being very brave.

"I know what to do!" Sky whizzed over the giant bubble. She looked very nervous, being so close to Jack Frost, and she whispered her spell so quietly that Rachel and Kirsty couldn't hear the words.

A jet of blue fairy dust streamed out of
Sky's wand and into the bubble. The dust
swirled in a spiral, bigger and bigger, until
it filled the whole bubble.

Rachel and Kirsty flew over and
peered in.

The fairy dust had turned into huge
crystal snowflakes. The water on Jack
Frost's face froze into tiny drops
of ice. He had stopped
melting! The wind whipped
the snow faster, spinning
around Jack Frost in circles.

"Look! He's getting smaller and smaller!" Kirsty gasped.

She was right. Now, Jack Frost was smaller than a goblin. Then, he was smaller than a squirrel, then, even smaller than Queenie the bee. Everyone looked from the bubble to Sky and back again. What was going to happen next?

With a loud *POP*, the bubble burst. The wind dropped and the snow vanished.

At first, Kirsty thought Jack Frost had completely disappeared. Then she caught sight of a very small glass dome lying on the grass. Inside the dome there was a tiny figure leaping around angrily.

48

"It's a snow dome!" Kirsty said in amazement. "And Jack Frost's trapped inside!"

Time for a Rainbow

"Hooray for Sky!" shouted Rachel.
"Now, Jack Frost can't hurt any of us,
and we can take him safely back to
Fairyland." She flew over and picked up
the snow dome. It felt smooth and cold,
and it trembled when Jack Frost jumped
around.

Bertram hopped toward Rachel. "I'll take care of that, Miss Rachel," he said.

Rachel was glad to hand over the snow dome.

"Into the pot, everybody!" shouted Inky. "It's time to go back to Fairyland!"

"Yippee!" yelled Amber, doing a backflip in midair. Heather waved her wand and the pot rolled fully upright, onto its four short legs. Rachel, Kirsty, and all the fairies flew inside. Bertram the frog climbed in after them. It was a little crammed, but Rachel and Kirsty were too excited to mind.

"Ready?" Ruby asked.

Her sisters nodded, looking very serious. The seven Rainbow Fairies raised their wands. There was a flash above them, like rainbow-colored fireworks. A fountain of sparks filled the pot with beautiful bold colors: red, orange, yellow, green, blue, indigo, and violet.

And then the brightest rainbow Rachel and Kirsty had ever seen soared upward into the clear blue sky.

With a *whoosh*, Bertram and the fairies shot out of the pot, carried on the rainbow like a giant wave. Rachel and Kirsty felt themselves zooming up the rainbow, too. Flowers, stars, leaves, tiny butterflies, inkdrops, and bubbles made of fairy dust fizzed and popped around them.

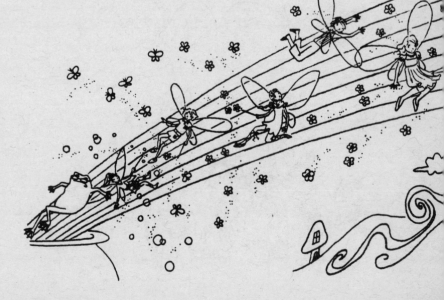

"This is amazing!" Kirsty shouted.

Far below, she could see hillsides dotted with toadstool houses. It was Fairyland! There was the winding river and the royal palace with its four pointed towers.

All of a sudden, the rainbow vanished in a fizz of fairy dust. Kirsty and Rachel flapped their wings and drifted gently to the ground. Rachel looked around, expecting to see all the colors coming back to Fairyland.

But the hills and the toadstool houses were still gray!

"Why hasn't the color returned?" Rachel gasped in horror.

Kirsty shrugged, too worried to speak.

One by one, the
Rainbow Fairies
landed softly next
to them. And
Kirsty saw that
where each fairy
had landed on the
gray grass, a patch of
the greenest green was
spreading outward.

"Rachel, look!" Kirsty
shouted. "The grass is turning
green!"

"Oh, yes!" Rachel said. Her eyes shone.

The fairy sisters stood in a circle and
raised their wands. A fountain of
rainbow-colored sparks shot up into the
fluffy, white clouds. There was a flash of
golden lightning, and it began to rain.

Rachel and Kirsty gazed in delight as tiny glittering raindrops, every color of the rainbow, pattered gently down around them. And where they fell, the color returned, flowing like shining paint across everything in Fairyland.

The toadstool
houses gleamed
red and white.
Brightly colored
flowers dotted the
green hillside with
orange, yellow, and purple.
Now, the river was the clearest blue.

On the highest hill, the fairy palace
shone softly pink. Music came out as the
front doors of the palace slowly opened.

Ruby flew down to Rachel and Kirsty.
"Hurry!" she said. "The king and queen
are waiting for us."

Rachel and Kirsty and the seven fairies
flew toward the palace. Below them,
Bertram hurried along with enormous
leaps.

The Rainbow Fairies beamed as elves, pixies, and fairies rushed out of the palace and danced around. "Hooray, hooray, for the Rainbow Fairies!" they cheered. "Hooray for Rachel and Kirsty!"

Titania and Oberon came out of the palace. The queen wore a silver dress and a sparkling diamond crown. The king's coat and crown were made of gold.

"Welcome back, dear Rainbow Fairies. We have missed you," said Titania, holding out her arms. "Thank you a thousand times, Rachel and Kirsty!"

Bertram gave a deep bow. "This is for you, Your Majesty," he said, giving the snow dome to Oberon.

"Thank you, Bertram," said Oberon. He held the snow dome in both hands and looked into it. "Now, Jack Frost," he said sternly. "If I let you out, will you promise to stay in your icy castle and not harm the Rainbow Fairies again?"

"Remember that winter still belongs to you," Titania reminded him.

Inside the snow dome, Jack Frost stroked his sharp chin. "Very well," he said. "But on one condition."

"And what is that?" asked Oberon.

Kirsty looked at Rachel, suddenly feeling worried. What was he going to ask for?

"That I'm invited to the next Midsummer Ball," said Jack Frost.

Titania smiled. "You will be very welcome," she said kindly.

Oberon tapped the snow dome and it cracked in half. Jack Frost sprang out and shot up to his full, bony height. Snow

glittered on his white
hair. He snapped his
fingers and a sleigh made
of ice appeared next to him.
Hopping onto it, he zoomed up
into the sky.

All the fairies waved.

"Good-bye. We'll see you next year
at the Midsummer Ball!" Sky called
after him.

Jack Frost looked over his shoulder. A
smile flickered across his sharp face. Then,
he was gone.

Very Special Gifts

The Fairy King and Queen smiled
warmly at Rachel and Kirsty.

"Thank you, dear friends," said
Oberon. "Without you, Jack Frost's spell
would never have been broken."

"You will always be welcome in
Fairyland," Titania told them. "And

wherever you go, watch for magic. It will always find you."

The Rainbow Fairies fluttered over to say good-bye. Rachel and Kirsty hugged them all in turn. They couldn't help feeling a bit sad. They were going to miss their new friends very much.

Bertram hopped over and shook their hands. "Good-bye, Miss Rachel and Miss Kirsty. It was a pleasure to meet you," he said.

"Now, here's a special rainbow to take you home!" said Heather.

The fairy sisters raised their wands one more time. An enormous shining rainbow whooshed upward, stretching all the way back to Rainspell Island.

"Here we go!" Rachel shouted with joy as she felt herself being sucked into the fizzing colors.

"I love riding on rainbows!" said Kirsty.

Soon the vacation cottages appeared below them. They landed in the backyard of Mermaid Cottage with a soft bump.

"Oh, we're back to our normal size," Rachel said, standing up.

"And we're just in time to catch the ferry!" Kirsty added as they ran around to the front yard.

"It's a shame our fairy adventures are over, isn't it?" Rachel said sadly.

Kirsty nodded. "But remember what Titania said about looking for magic from now on!"

"There you are," said Rachel's mom. "Did you see that beautiful rainbow? And it wasn't even raining. Rainspell Island is a really special place!"

Kirsty and Rachel shared a secret smile.

"The car's packed. Check your bedroom to see if you've left anything behind," said Kirsty's mom.

Kirsty dashed into Dolphin Cottage and went upstairs.

"I'll check mine, too!" Rachel hurried into Mermaid Cottage and ran upstairs to her little attic room for one last time. She stopped dead in her bedroom doorway. "Oh!" she gasped.

In the middle of the bed, something shone and glittered like a huge diamond. Rachel went closer. It was a snow dome, full of fluttering fairy-dust shapes in all the colors of the rainbow. "It's the most beautiful thing I've ever seen," Rachel said. She scooped up the glass dome and dashed next door.

Kirsty was running down the stairs. In her hands she held an identical snow dome. "I'm going to keep this forever!" she said.

The two friends beamed at each other. "Every time I shake my snow dome, or see a rainbow, it will make me think of Fairyland and all the Rainbow Fairies," said Rachel as they left the cottage.

"Me, too!" replied Kirsty. "We'll *never* forget our secret fairy friends."

"No, we won't," said Rachel. "*Never.*"